STEP 1
READY TO READ

SOCCER TIME!

by Terry Pierce

illustrated by Bob McMahon

Random House New York

Soccer time!

We get in line.

We start with drills.

But some take spills.

We run on grass

and kick to pass.

No hands—just feet.

The game starts.

Tweet!

I dribble.

Tap!

The fans all clap.

Kids block the ball.

Some take a fall.

The coaches shout,

"Spread out!"

"Spread out!"

We pass.

We trap.

We see a gap.

I dribble lots.
I take a shot!

The goalie falls . . .

... but stops the ball!

"Just try again!"
our coach shouts in.

23

I get it back.

I kick it.

<u>Smack!</u>

Tap left, kick left.

<u>Tweet!</u> blasts the ref.

We kick.
We play.

"Hey!

Not that way!"

I kick.
It rolls.

I score a goal!

Our game is done.

We all had fun.

We make a line.

Bye, soccer time!

Dear Parents:

Congratulations! Your child is taking the first steps on an exciting journey. The destination? Independent reading!

STEP INTO READING® will help your child get there. The program offers five steps to reading success. Each step includes fun stories and colorful art or photographs. In addition to original fiction and books with favorite characters, there are Step into Reading Non-Fiction Readers, Phonics Readers and Boxed Sets, Sticker Readers, and Comic Readers—a complete literacy program with something to interest every child.

Learning to Read, Step by Step!

Ready to Read   Preschool–Kindergarten
• big type and easy words • rhyme and rhythm • picture clues
For children who know the alphabet and are eager to begin reading.

Reading with Help   Preschool–Grade 1
• basic vocabulary • short sentences • simple stories
For children who recognize familiar words and sound out new words with help.

Reading on Your Own   Grades 1–3
• engaging characters • easy-to-follow plots • popular topics
For children who are ready to read on their own.

Reading Paragraphs   Grades 2–3
• challenging vocabulary • short paragraphs • exciting stories
For newly independent readers who read simple sentences with confidence.

Ready for Chapters   Grades 2–4
• chapters • longer paragraphs • full-color art
For children who want to take the plunge into chapter books but still like colorful pictures.

STEP INTO READING® is designed to give every child a successful reading experience. The grade levels are only guides; children will progress through the steps at their own speed, developing confidence in their reading. The F&P Text Level on the back cover serves as another tool to help you choose the right book for your child.

Remember, a lifetime love of reading starts with a single step!

To Stacey, Megan, Pete, and Bayne,
with much thanks—GOOOAAALLL!
—T.P.

To my own champions Tyler and Lalane
—B.M.

Text copyright © 2019 by Terry Pierce
Cover art and interior illustrations copyright © 2019 by Bob McMahon

All rights reserved. Published in the United States by Random House Children's Books,
a division of Penguin Random House LLC, New York.

Step into Reading, Random House, and the Random House colophon
are registered trademarks of Penguin Random House LLC.

Visit us on the Web!
StepIntoReading.com
rhcbooks.com

Educators and librarians, for a variety of teaching tools,
visit us at RHTeachersLibrarians.com

Library of Congress Cataloging-in-Publication Data
Names: Pierce, Terry, author. | McMahon, Bob, illustrator.
Title: Soccer time! / by Terry Pierce; illustrated by Bob McMahon.
Description: New York: Random House, [2019] | Series: Step into reading. Step 1 |
Summary: In rhyming verse, active children learn the fundamentals of soccer.
Identifiers: LCCN 2018037169 | ISBN 978-0-525-58203-8 (pbk.) |
ISBN 978-0-525-58204-5 (lib. bdg.) |. ISBN 978-0-525-58205-2 (ebook)
Subjects: | CYAC: Stories in rhyme. | Soccer—Fiction.
Classification: LCC PZ8.3.P558643 So 2019 | DDC [E]—dc23

MANUFACTURED IN CHINA
10 9 8 7 6 5 4 3

This book has been officially leveled by using the F&P Text Level Gradient™ Leveling System.